Full STEAM Ahead!

Arts in Action

The Five Parts of Art

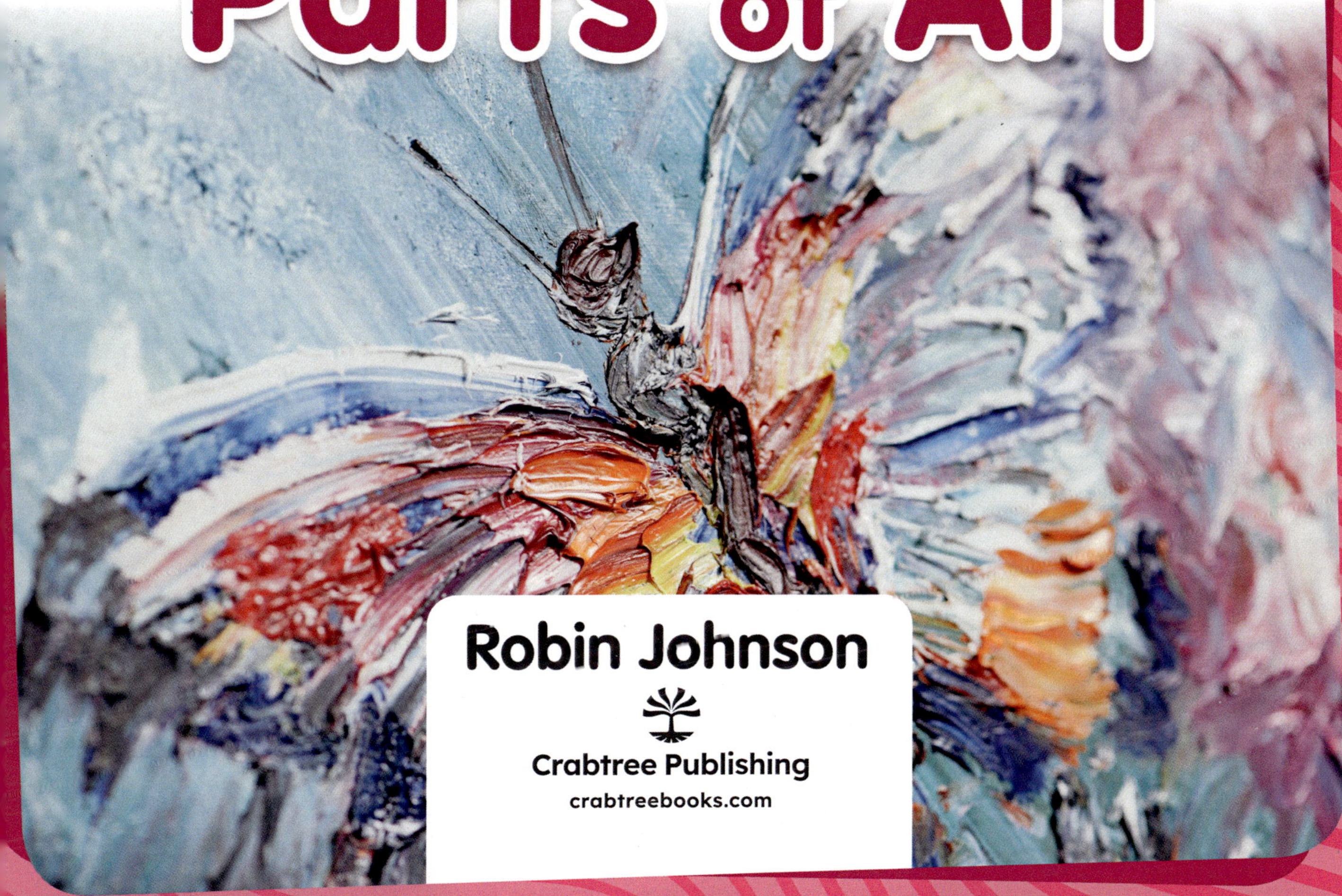

Robin Johnson

Crabtree Publishing
crabtreebooks.com

Title-Specific Learning Objectives:
Readers will:

- Identify the five parts of art and explain how each part has a purpose.
- Explain how the five parts of art work together.
- Find information provided in images and information provided in text.

High-frequency words (grade one) a, are, at, can, for, is, make, the, there, this	**Academic vocabulary** color, line, mosaic, pattern, pottery wheel, sculpture, shape, space, texture

Before, During, and After Reading Prompts:

Activate Prior Knowledge and Make Predictions:
Have children read the title and look at the images on the cover and title page. Ask them:

- What do you think this book will be about?
- Do you know any of the five parts of art?
- Can you see any parts of art in the images on the cover or title page?

During Reading:
After reading pages 6 and 7, ask children to re-read the five parts of art, then look at the images that show each part. Finally, look at the images on page 7 that show multiple parts together. Ask them:

- What information do you get from the words? What information do you get from the images? Is the information the same? How is it different?

After Reading:
Create an anchor chart with words and definitions for the five parts of art. Have children come up with definitions themselves. Invite children to create art that displays each part. Create a "Parts of Art" wall with the anchor chart and accompanying art.

Author: Robin Johnson

Series Development: Reagan Miller

Editor: Janine Deschenes

Proofreader: Melissa Boyce

STEAM Notes for Educators: Janine Deschenes

Guided Reading Leveling: Publishing Solutions Group

Cover, Interior Design, and Prepress: Samara Parent

Photo research: Robin Johnson and Samara Parent
Production coordinator: Katherine Kantor
Photographs:
Shutterstock: Sopha Changaroon: cover; BestPhotoPlus: p. 4; Darkdiamond67: p. 5 (t); meunierd: p. 10 (br); CJM Grafx: p. 13 (t); Pyty: p. 13 (b); Comaniciu Dan: p. 15 (l); SUPREEYA-ANON: p. 17 (b); pio3: p. 19 (t); Rolf G Wackenberg: p. 20; manzrussali: p. 21
All other photographs by Shutterstock

Library and Archives Canada Cataloguing in Publication

Title: The five parts of art / Robin Johnson.
Names: Johnson, Robin (Robin R.), author.
Description: Series statement: Full STEAM ahead! | Includes index.
Identifiers: Canadiana (print) 20190133562 |
Canadiana (ebook) 20190133589 |
ISBN 9780778764618 (softcover) |
ISBN 9780778764366 (hardcover) |
ISBN 9781427123633 (HTML)
Subjects: LCSH: Art—Technique—Juvenile literature. |
LCSH: Composition (Art)—Juvenile literature.
Classification: LCC N7430 .J64 2019 | DDC j701/.1—dc23

Library of Congress Cataloging-in-Publication Data

Names: Johnson, Robin (Robin R.) author.
Title: The five parts of art / Robin Johnson.
Description: New York, New York : Crabtree Publishing Company, 2019. Series: Full STEAM ahead! | Includes index.
Identifiers: LCCN 2019026388 (print) | LCCN 2019026389 (ebook) |
ISBN 9780778764366 (hardcover) |
ISBN 9780778764618 (paperback) |
ISBN 9781427123633 (ebook)
Subjects: LCSH: Composition (Art)--Juvenile literature.
Classification: LCC N7430 .J58 2019 (print) | LCC N7430 (ebook) |
DDC 701/.8--dc23
LC record available at https://lccn.loc.gov/2019026388
LC ebook record available at https://lccn.loc.gov/2019026389

Table of Contents

Crabtree Publishing

crabtreebooks.com 800-387-7650

Published in Canada
Crabtree Publishing
616 Welland Avenue
St. Catharines, Ontario
L2M 5V6

Published in the United States
Crabtree Publishing
347 Fifth Avenue
Suite 1402-145
New York, NY 10016

Printed in Canada/012025/CP20250101

What is Art?

There are many kinds of art. Some types of art are things that people can look at. Artists make beautiful pictures. They make interesting **sculptures** and colorful clothing.

This boy is looking at paintings. This type of art is made for people to look at and enjoy.

These baskets have lines, color, shape, space, and texture.

Can you see the five parts of art on these pieces of stained-glass art?

Artists Use Lines

Lines are marks that artists make on art. Lines show the edges or outlines of objects. They let us see the shapes artists make. There are many kinds of lines.

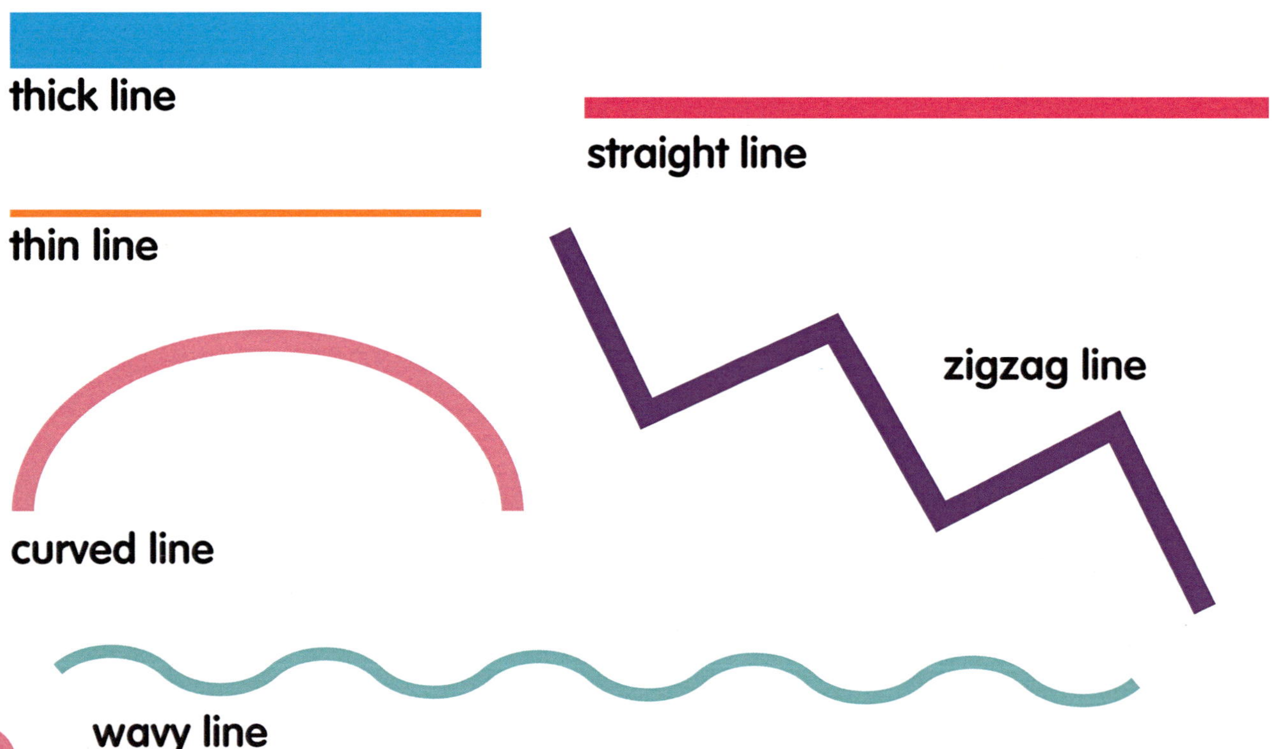

This artist uses straight lines and curved lines to draw different shapes.

An artist used wavy lines to paint the ocean. The wavy lines show that the water is moving.

Artists Use Color

Artists use color to show different feelings. Bright colors can show happy feelings. Dark colors can show sad feelings. Color can also make parts of art stand out.

An artist used dark colors to show this man is sad.

An artist used bright colors to show these people are happy.

An artist added the color red to this photo. The color makes the bicycle stand out.

An artist made this picture on a computer. Using a black background makes the other colors stand out.

Artists Use Shape

Shape is the form or outline of an object. Squares and circles are shapes. Stars and flowers are shapes too. Artists use different shapes to make their art interesting.

This beautiful **mosaic** is made of pieces with different shapes. An artist put the pieces together to make new shapes.

This building has a shape like a giant basket. The shape makes it interesting to look at.

An artist put different shapes together to make this sculpture.

Artists Use Space

Space is the area in and around objects. Artists use space to make people and places look real. They also use space to draw your eyes to certain parts of the art.

An artist used space to make this painting look real. The large people at the bottom of the picture look close to us. The small houses at the top of the picture look far away.

An artist used empty space to make this sculpture interesting.

There is a lot of empty space around the girl in this photo. The space draws your eyes to the girl.

Artists Use Texture

Texture is the look or feel of a **surface**. Art can be smooth or rough. It can be hard or soft. Artists use texture to make their art look real or interesting.

An artist used paint to make this picture have a rough texture. Can you see the raised spots of paint?

Artists can make texture you can feel. They can also make art that looks like it has texture. The lines on this fish make its body look like it has texture.

This sculpture has a smooth, shiny texture. It **reflects** people and buildings around it.

Making Patterns

Artists can use the five parts of art to make **patterns**. They repeat lines, colors, shapes, spaces, or textures in their art.

Artists used the five parts of art to make many different patterns on these bowls.

Lines and shapes repeat on this sculpture.

An artist is **weaving** a pattern into this cloth. They repeat colors to make the pattern.

All Together Now

Artists put the five parts of art together. They use the parts to make art that is interesting and beautiful.

The shape, lines, and texture of this sculpture make it look like a real rabbit. Its pink color and huge space make it look interesting!

A mural is a picture painted directly on a wall. How do the five parts of art work together in this mural?

Words to Know

mosaic [moh-ZEY-ik] noun Art made of many small pieces

pattern [PAT-ern] noun A repeated design

reflect [ri-FLEKT] verb To give back an image

sculptures [SKUHLP-chers] noun Art made by shaping and putting together materials

surface [SUR-fis] noun The outside or top of something

texture [TEKS-cher] noun The feel or appearance of a surface

vase [veys] noun A tall container mostly used for decoration or to hold flowers

weaving [weev-ing] verb Lacing together pieces of fabric

A noun is a person, place, or thing.

A verb is an action word that tells you what someone or something does.

An adjective is a word that tells you what something is like.

Index

About the Author

Robin Johnson is a freelance author and editor who has written more than 80 children's books. When she isn't working, Robin builds castles in the sky with her engineer husband and their two best creations—sons Jeremy and Drew.

STEAM Notes for Educators

Full STEAM Ahead is a literacy series that helps readers build vocabulary, fluency, and comprehension while learning about big ideas in STEAM subjects. *The Five Parts of Art* introduces readers to visual art techniques while allowing them to gather and differentiate between information in images and text. The STEAM activity below helps readers extend the ideas in the book to build their skills in arts and math.

My Art Pattern

Children will be able to:

- Make an art piece that clearly includes the five parts of art.
- Use the parts of art to make a repeating pattern. (Extension: the pattern can include 2-D or 3-D shapes.)

Materials

- Art materials and tools, including sponges, craft sticks, paper, rulers, tape, glue, brushes, feathers, paint, clay, pencils, crayons, stones, petals, plastic blocks or toys, canvas, etc.
- My Art Pattern Worksheet
- Sticky notes

Guiding Prompts

After reading *The Five Parts of Art*, ask:

- What are the five parts of art? Create a child-centered definition for each. Review some art in the book to show examples of the five parts.
- Review pages 18 and 19. Ask children: What is a pattern? How do the parts of art help us make patterns?

Activity Prompts

Explain to children that they will use the five parts of art to create artwork with a pattern. If children have studied 2-D and 3-D shapes, their pattern can also incorporate these.

Hand each child the My Art Pattern Worksheet. Explain that they need to use the worksheet to plan their artwork. Review the criteria with them: their artwork must show the five parts of art. Conference with children as they work, to ensure they are on the right path.

Have children complete their artwork after their worksheets are finished. Then, display the artwork. Hand each child 5 sticky notes. They should use the sticky notes to label each of the five parts of art in their artwork.

Extensions

- Invite children to experiment with one of the parts of art to change the feel of their artwork. They should change something about one part, such as changing straight lines to wavy. Discuss how this changes the look or feel of their artwork.

To view and download the worksheet, visit **www.crabtreebooks.com/resources/printables**